THE Ghost Child

Emma Child

Emma Tennant

Illustrated by
CHARLOTTE VOAKE

HEINEMANN:LONDON

For Rose

William Heinemann Ltd
10 Upper Grosvenor Street, London W1X 9 PA

LONDON · MELBOURNE · TORONTO
JOHANNESBURG · AUCKLAND

First published 1984, Reprinted 1985
Text © Emma Tennant 1984
Illustrations © Charlotte Voake 1984

A school pack of BANANAS 1–6
is available from
Heinemann Educational Books
ISBN 0 435 00100 0

434 93025 3
Printed in Hong Kong by
Imago Publishing Ltd

MELLY NEVER LIKED the last day of summer term. Everyone else in Class 6 seemed to have exciting plans for the holidays. Melly's friend Anna was going to France. She said the sea was so blue there you could dive all day. Her friend Jane was going to work as a stable-hand in a real stables. She'd be allowed to ride the horses, too. Only Becca, who was younger than Melly and lived next door, was always in London when Melly came back from her fortnight at Grandma's.

This summer even Becca had a holiday plan.

1

'But where exactly are you going?' Melly said. The school bell had just rung and desk lids were banging down until the beginning of a whole new term.

Becca wouldn't answer. She'd already boasted she was going to America but all the other children laughed when she said it was "Dizzy-world" in America where she was going. No one believed Becca any more. But no one even bothered to ask Melly where she was going. This was because Melly's holiday was always the same. There was the train journey over flat country to her grandparents' house,

2

the guard who passed in the corridor as she stared out at yellow fields and big churches, and the sight of Grandpa in his stubby car by the station gate. Then there was a fortnight with nothing much to do. Melly never brought back exciting news.

'Let's walk home together,' Melly said to Becca.

All the children were going off whistling and singing down the long street outside the school.

Becca and Melly nearly always walked

home together. Becca's brothers, the Brown boys, played football after school or went to tea with friends. The walk was more fun when you could play at going all the way home without treading on a crack in the pavement – or at shouting a word to make up the letters on a car number-plate.

'CAKE,' Becca called when a postman's van with a CK went by.

Becca had just had a birthday. Melly didn't laugh today, though. She walked on thoughtfully without even noticing the cracks in the stones where she put her feet.

'AWFUL,' Melly said, as a black car with AFL on the number-plate passed them in the street. 'I wish I was going away somewhere nice, like you are,' she said. 'But where *are* you going, Becca? I won't tell anyone, I promise.'

Still Becca wouldn't answer. She skipped happily up to her front gate. Mrs Brown waved from the window. 'Come in and have some tea, Melly,' she said.

'Your mum rang and said she was going to be late home from work tonight.'

'Thanks very much,' Melly said. She felt sadder than ever as she went into the Browns' cheerful house. Surely her mum could have come home early

tonight, the first night of the holidays?
Melly was going to her grandparents'
tomorrow; she'd hardly have time to
see her mum at all.

'You know how hard your mum
works,' Mrs Brown said, as if she'd
guessed what Melly was thinking. 'Have
some blackberry jelly with the crumpets.
We picked them when we went out to
the country last summer. Do you
remember, Becca?'

Melly felt a little better when she'd eaten the crumpets and cake. So she said teasingly to Becca, 'You know, I don't believe you're going anywhere at all in the holidays. You'll just go blackberrying again for a few days, like you did last year.'

'No, no,' Mrs Brown said, and she was laughing. 'Something quite new is going to happen to Becca. It's just that she's not allowed yet to know what it is.'

And then the Brown boys came back and there was a terrible clatter of footballs and boots in the hall. Melly played cards with Becca until her mum came and banged on the door and Melly and her mum walked the few steps down the road to their home.

The next day everything went as it always did on the first day of the summer holidays. There was the long train journey, and there was Grandpa in his

funny old-fashioned car. There was the
drive to the house with the car groaning
and rattling whenever the road was
rough. There was Grandma, snipping at
roses in the front garden and coming
forward with her arms open, ready for a
hug.

Inside, it was just the same as last time. There were the stairs, with the pictures of ships on stormy seas all the way up the walls. There was the landing, with the brown stain where Melly had once dropped a glass of painting water. Melly walked up without bothering to look where she was going. She knew it all so well.

But this time something was different. Melly didn't notice at first that a door was open at the top of the stairs, and that it was a door to a room she'd never been in before. She walked right past the door without even looking in, and by the time she came down for supper it was closed again.

When supper was over, Melly said she would go for a short walk. She felt lonely and bored already. Grandpa and Grandma were very nice but there was no one of her own age for miles around to play with. 'I'd rather be on my own,' she said, when Grandpa offered to come too. And she set off out into the garden where night was falling and there were long shadows under the trees.

It was when Melly looked back at the

house from the garden that she had her
first surprise. A light was on upstairs,
and she knew it wasn't her light, which
would have glowed in the red curtains in
her room. It couldn't be Grandma's
bedroom light either.

Suddenly, Melly felt frightened,
standing in the garden that was dark by
now and looking up at a square of light in
a room that wasn't really there. 'Yes,
that's my room,' a voice said, just behind
Melly. 'I always leave my light on at
night so I can find my way back.'

Melly swung round. Her heart was thumping. But the boy who now faced her didn't seem rough or rude like Becca's brothers, the Brown boys. He had very neat hair, Melly saw, with a side parting. And he wore a strange-looking school blazer. But his face was nice, and he was smiling. 'D'you want to see some athletics?' the boy said. 'I'll teach you anything you don't know already.'

Now if there was one thing Melly really liked it was going to the gym. She always wished she could spend longer there and not have to go back in to lessons. 'Yes please,' Melly said. Then, 'What's your name?' she asked shyly.

But the boy had already run ahead. He stood on a patch of lawn that was smooth and pale in the moonlight. And he beckoned to Melly to come and join him, before cartwheeling lightly over the grass.

Melly couldn't remember when she had last enjoyed herself so much. The lawn was slightly damp and smelt deliciously mossy, as she followed the boy on his tour of acrobatics. Soon she had caught up with him and he was clapping his hands and laughing. Melly

did shoulder-stands; head-stands; teddy rolls; crabs; double back somersaults. When she stopped for a rest, he ran up and she could see how pleased he was to be with her.

'So many new things since my day,' he said. 'It's exciting. I expect you'll be asked to do stunts in a film,' he went on. Melly thought he sounded wistful. 'The films they made when I was a child weren't as exciting as they are today, you know.'

'But you are a child,' Melly burst out. 'I mean – who are you? Please tell me.'

'I'm Rick,' the boy said. 'I'm your Grandpa's brother. And they keep my room for me just as it always was when our mother and father were alive and looked after us here.'

'Alive?' Melly said before she could stop herself.

Because of course Rick couldn't be
alive. He'd be an old man like Grandpa
by now.

'Come on, let's have a cartwheel race,'
Rick said before Melly could think any
more. 'Beat you to the last tree over
there by the house.'

That was how Melly found herself in the room she'd never seen before. It was all a bit like a dream, really. One minute she was in the garden on the pale grass lit up by the moon.

Then everything seemed to go very quiet while Rick opened the door. They climbed the stairs without making any noise at all.

'I didn't die when I was a boy,' Rick said, as if he knew how to read Melly's thoughts. They were standing in his room now, which was filled with silver cups and certificates: Melly could see

that Rick must have been *very* good at
games. 'I was killed in the last war,' Rick
explained, 'before your mum was even
born. I was a pilot in a fighter plane, and I
was shot down over Germany.'

'Why, then . . .' Melly began.

'I come back here as a boy because
your Grandpa keeps my room for me just
as it was,' Rick said. 'And because I was
happy here. Look at my butterfly
collection, Melly.'

But Melly had picked up a big silver

cup. 'What a lovely cup, Rick,' she said. 'Was this for gym or sports?'

'Oh, that one,' Rick said as if he couldn't care less. But he looked rather pleased. 'That was the swimming gala. High-diving and front crawl, actually.'

'High-diving!' Melly exclaimed. 'That's something I've always wanted to do!'

'Very well,' Rick said. 'If you meet me tomorrow night in the garden I'll show you how.'

'But there isn't a pool in the garden,' Melly said.

'Wait and see,' said Rick. Then he put his hand on her shoulder and said softly, 'Do you hear the clock, Melly? It's midnight. You must go.'

And Melly knew, as she walked out of Rick's room, that she mustn't look back. Rick's room wouldn't be there.

The next day Melly went out on the
landing early but even the door to Rick's
room had gone. There was just the old

wallpaper, the same as it had always been.

The day seemed to go on forever, until it was time for supper – and there was Grandpa in his chair, drinking his soup noisily, as he always did.

'Grandpa?' Melly said.

'Mmm . . .' replied Grandpa between slurping sounds.

'Is . . . is there, I mean was there, a little boy here called Rick?'

'Rick?' Grandpa looked up, surprised. 'Yes, Melly, my dear. He was my younger brother. Why do you ask? Did he come to see you?'

'Yes,' Melly said. 'Last night.'

'And he'll want so much to come tonight,' Grandpa said. He shook his head sadly. 'Poor Rick.'

'Why? Why poor Rick?' Melly suddenly felt that she didn't want to hear

what Grandpa was going to say next.

'Rick comes back for just one night every year,' Grandpa said. 'Last night was the same date as the night he was killed, you see.'

'Oh,' Melly said. 'So I won't see Rick again?'

'Maybe next year,' Grandpa said in a kind voice. He finished his soup and Grandma brought in cheese on toast. 'You were lucky he chose you this time,' Grandpa said, while Grandma nodded at Melly and smiled. 'He usually says hello to us and goes off to his room to see his

butterfly collection and his stamp collection. I always try to put in the most up-to-date stamps for him.' Grandpa smiled. 'He must have taken a real liking to you,' he said.

Melly didn't feel sleepy that night. When Grandma said, 'Bedtime, Melly,' she only pretended to go to her room and put on her pyjamas. Because of course she didn't believe she would never see Rick again. She knew he'd be in the garden, waiting for her.

He wasn't, though. The moon was full out in the garden—and at first every shadow under every tree seemed to be Rick. But when Melly got closer there was just dark grass, with a coating of dew that had come up in the night.

Melly walked along the path and on to

the wide lawn where she and Rick had done their headstands and cartwheels.

As she went, she felt her body grow lighter and a faint breeze play on her shoulders and neck. And when Melly looked down, she saw she was wearing a black swimsuit. The lawn ahead of her glittered in the moonlight. But now it was real water that shone there under the moon. It wasn't just dew on the grass.

The lawn had become a great pool—Melly could even see the diving-board, sticking out at the end of the pool from under the trees. 'Now, Melly,' a voice said quietly. 'Just walk to the end of the pool. You're going to do a perfect dive.'

Melly swung round quickly. It was Rick's voice she had heard—so he had come after all! She could feel herself smiling, alone in the shadowy garden.

But Rick wasn't there. Melly walked the length of the pool, wondering when he would come out of the trees. She knew she would never dare try her first high-dive all on her own.

'Climb up there,' the voice said when Melly reached the diving-board. 'I'm sorry, Melly, I can't be with you tonight. But just think—if you dive really well, I'll give you my silver cup to take home!'

Melly thought she had never been so scared in her life. She climbed up to the high board and shivered when she looked down.

'Now raise your arms,' Rick's voice said. 'And duck your head.'

'I can't do it!' Melly said. Her voice echoed round the empty garden. 'I really can't!'

But as she spoke, there came a faint push on her shoulders, and Melly's arms went forward and her head ducked. Now she was falling, falling, to the water far below.

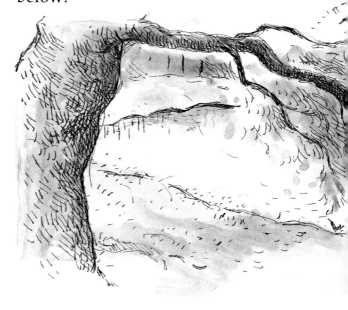

'That was a perfect dive,' Rick's voice was calling excitedly as Melly swam to the surface and looked over the edge of the pool at the moon-dappled grass. 'Well done, Melly! Now for a double somersault!'

If anyone had told Melly at the end of term that she'd be able to dive like this, she'd have laughed at them. Backwards somersaults, even turning three times in mid-air. She could have gone on diving forever.

But—'That's enough for now, Melly,' Rick's voice said. 'Go back to the house and you'll find the silver cup in your room!'

'Rick?' Melly said as she walked away from the pool and along the path.

'Yes, Melly. What is it?' Rick's voice sounded further away now, and Melly saw she was in her jeans and sweatshirt again. They rubbed her legs and arms a bit, as clothes do when you haven't had time to get dry.

'Rick, could you come and see me in London?'

There was silence at first. It was only as Melly opened the garden door that Rick's voice came, so faint it could have been no more than the sigh of the wind in the leaves. 'Perhaps I will, Melly. But it won't be the same.'

When it was time to go home, Melly promised herself on the train that she wouldn't tell anybody about Rick, not even Becca or Mum.

But it was a hard promise to keep. Grandma had packed the silver cup Rick had given her for the high-dive. Mum saw it when she unpacked. Melly said Grandpa had given it to her. Mum didn't look as if she believed that at all. But Melly liked remembering Grandma's

special smile when she wrapped the cup in tissue paper and put it in the bottom of the case. Grandpa and Grandma knew Rick had come to play, even if Mum was too busy usually to make the secret worth telling.

At least Becca was away. That was lucky, Melly thought, or she might have had to tell her about Rick. She didn't even wonder where Becca had gone.

Three days after Melly got back, there was a big thunderstorm. Melly's mum came back early from work and said the thunder had given her a headache so she was going to bed. And Melly sat alone in her room, looking out at the lightning that suddenly lit up the row of small gardens at the back of the houses. The thunder was like planes zooming about in the sky.

She couldn't sleep so she went to the window to look out. At first Melly couldn't believe her eyes. There *were* planes, not jumbos but small planes – fighter planes, some of them burning up in the air, others falling into the dark gardens. There was fire and noise everywhere, like a Guy Fawkes night gone mad. Melly stared and stared.

The lights in Becca's house went on.
So she must be back from her holiday.
But Melly hardly noticed. She was
staring down at her own garden now,
where the lightning coming and going
made a jerky picture, like the
black-and-white films Rick would have
seen when he was a boy.

A man was standing in the garden.
Flames flickered round him, from the
body of a crashed plane. He looked up at

Melly and he suddenly seemed very near, as if he'd come right up to the windowsill.

'Hello, Melly,' the man said.

Melly didn't know what to say, but she couldn't stop looking out.

'You see,' the man said, 'I told you it wouldn't be the same if I came to see you in London.'

'Rick,' Melly whispered. She didn't dare look much longer at this handsome young man with a funny little moustache and kind eyes. 'Why –' she began.

'London was my home when I grew up,' Rick said. 'I can only be a little boy in the country, Melly.'

'You've got two ghosts then, Uncle Rick,' Melly said quietly.

'Yes,' Rick said. 'But I like coming back as a child. It's so much more fun!'

'You'll come and see me next summer in the holidays, please promise you will,' Melly said.

But already the thunder and lightning were fading away and Melly couldn't see Uncle Rick any more.

'You know I will,' a voice said as she climbed back into bed.

Becca was very excited the next day about the thunderstorm.

'We came home in the middle of it,' she boasted.

'Yes, I saw it too,' Melly said. She smiled. She would never tell Becca now about Rick and his two ghosts.

'Where did you have your holiday?' Melly asked Becca. 'Did you get to Dizzy-World?' And Melly thought that nothing as new as what had happened to her could possibly have happened to Becca.

'It was a surprise,' Becca said. 'I didn't go outside London at all. But my Mum went into hospital and I went to stay with my auntie and the next day I went to see my new baby brother!'

'Oh, Becca!' Melly said. She was happy for Becca, but she had Rick's visit next summer to look forward to.

'Did you have a nice holiday, Melly?' Becca asked.

'Oh, yes, very,' Melly said.

'Don't you wish you had a new baby brother?' Becca said.

Melly still didn't tell Becca about Rick. 'Yes, I wish I had a real brother,' Melly said. Then she thought of the Brown boys. And she added kindly, 'I'm sure this baby won't grow up to be like your other brothers, Becca!'